Also by Jon Blake,
published by Hodder Children's Books:

The Deadly Secret of Dorothy W.
The Mad Mission of Jasmin J.

And coming soon, more adventures
with Stinky and friends:

Crazy Party at the House of Fun
Mystery Guest at the House of Fun

Jon Blake

illustrated by
David Roberts

*Hodder
Children's
Books*

A division of Hodder Headline Limited

Before We Begin

First let me introduce myself. I am Blue Soup. I tell stories. I also light up cities, provide hot dinners, and make that little thing in the top of the toilet go FZZZZZZZ. In fact, I make everything work, so no one has to waste their time being a cleaner, or an estate agent, or an MP.

What am I, you ask? Well, I'm not a person, that's obvious. Or a team of people. Or a computer virus. But please don't waste your time trying to imagine me, because you can't, just like you can't imagine the end of time, or what's beyond the very last star. If you do try to imagine me, first you will get a headache, then your head will explode.

As you've probably guessed, I come from Outer Space. Beyond the very last star, in fact. I was brought here by what you call aliens, except to them, you are aliens, and pretty weird ones at that.

Anyway, enough of me. This is the story of Stinky Finger, who definitely isn't an alien. He talks like a human, and walks like a human, and smells like a dead fish.

Warning

This story starts quite slow and calm, then gets increasingly mad. A diagram of the story would look like this:

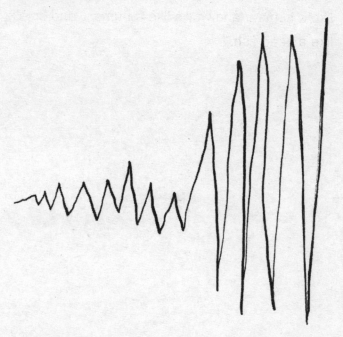

This story is not suitable for humans over the age of eighteen or for anyone with a fear of pigs.

Chapter One

Stinky Finger and Icky Bats sat on two tree stumps at the edge of the silver forest, looking down at the snow-covered city. They were thinking about the days before the Spoonheads arrived in their spacehoovers and sucked up all the grown-ups.

"I miss Mum and Dad sometimes," said Icky.

"I don't," replied Stinky. "They were always going on at me. Every single Christmas they made me change my undies."

"What's wrong with that?" asked Icky.

"I'm very attached to my undies," replied Stinky.

"That's because of the mould and fungus," said Icky.

This was very true. There was a lot of mould and fungus in Stinky's undies, but not as much as there used to be, because little animals had moved in and eaten most of it. Only Icky Bats could stand the stink of Stinky Finger. A cricket ball had smacked Icky on the nose and destroyed his sense of smell.

"I miss my Uncle Jav as well," said Icky.

"Yes, he wasn't too bad," admitted Stinky. "He didn't deserve to be sucked into the Spoonheads' space zoo for all eternity."

"He gave me this," said Icky, pulling out a feather.

"That's nice," said Stinky.

"It's a lucky feather," said Icky. "He said it might save my life one day."

Stinky looked hard at the feather. "How do you think a feather could save your life?" he asked.

Icky thought about this for a while, but he never thought about anything for long. "Did you have any uncles, Stinky?" he asked.

"Not exactly," replied Stinky.

"How can you not exactly have an uncle?" asked Icky.

"There *was* Uncle Nero," replied Stinky, "but he was just a head."

"Just a *head?*" repeated Icky.

"He was very sick," explained Stinky, "so he had his head frozen and connected to the Internet, or something."

"Did it still work?" asked Icky.

"I think so," replied Stinky.

Icky looked out over the fresh white city, his mind alive with thoughts. "If the Spoonheads sucked up all the grown-ups," he mused, "did that include your uncle's head?"

"I don't know," said Stinky. "I never thought about it."

"Let's find out!" shouted Icky, jumping to his feet.

Stinky wasn't so sure. He could always think of ten thousand reasons not to do anything.

"Can't we just stay here?" he said.

"Stinky," said Icky, "we've been sitting here for three weeks. We've got to have an Aim In Life."

That was true. Now that school had closed down and Blue Soup ran everything, there was no particular need to get out of bed in the morning. With no grown-ups around, there wasn't even any point in causing trouble. If you didn't invent your own Aim In Life, then life was a bit like ... well, death.

"OK," said Stinky. He tried to rise, but the gubbins on his trousers had mingled with the gubbins on the tree stump, and he was stuck fast. Icky kept a small saw for accidents like this, so they were able to get Stinky up, with a thin circle of tree still stuck to his backside. Luckily this blended in with all the other rubbish hanging from his clothes.

The two great mates set off down the hill towards the city. They weren't exactly sure where they were going, but they did know that Uncle

Nero had lived somewhere near the council tip, and the council tip was somewhere near the old flea market, and the old flea market was somewhere near the pet cemetery.

If only they knew where the pet cemetery was. Or if it still existed. The Spoonheads had moved quite a few things around, sometimes for no reason at all.

"If we had a map it would help," said Icky.

"If we could read maps it would be even better," added Stinky.

Suddenly Icky and Stinky stopped dead. Ahead of them was a giant video screen:

Icky and Stinky gaped at the huge smarmy face on the screen. Bryan Brain had been the brainiest boy in their class at school, but this was the first time they had seen what he looked like. That was because they had been taught in a very long thin classroom, only slightly wider than a desk. Bryan Brain sat at the very front of it, and Icky and Stinky sat at the very back. That was because Bryan Brain always came top in the weekly test, and Icky and Stinky always came bottom. Icky was always messing about, and Stinky could never get past the first question, which was "What is the date today?"

"Are you thinking what I'm thinking?" asked Icky.

"Only if you're thinking nothing," said Stinky.

"Bryan Brain will know where the pet cemetery is!" said Icky.

"Oh yes!" said Stinky.

"Let's get down the TV studio," said Icky, "and arrest him or something."

Icky and Stinky quickened their step. They did know where the TV studio was, because the Spoonheads had decided that every kid on earth

should have fifty-three seconds of fame. Icky had
appeared on a show called Small Lively Boys, and
Stinky had starred in Stench Academy. Shortly
after, they and a hundred other kids had appeared
in Celebkid magazine, in a photo the size of a
postage stamp.

Note from Blue Soup:
Bryan Brain had no chance of winning 'real'
money in the competition. The Spoonheads had
abolished all 'real' money, as I (Blue Soup)
provided for everybody's needs and 'real' money
was therefore pointless.

Town looked fantastically exciting in its blanket of
snow. Little footsteps criss-crossed the roadways,
none bigger than a size 5 (continental size 38).
Starlings fought over frozen pork pie crusts. Russell
Goody sailed past on a golden sledge, giving the
boys a regal wave. After the Spoonheads had left
he had decided to crown himself king, but no one
took much notice.

Just as they turned into the Old Market Square,
a nervous frown came over Stinky. Up ahead a

gang of dogs were lounging around by the bubble fountains. Catching the scent of Stinky (which wasn't difficult) they looked up.

"Don't look at them," advised Stinky.

This, of course, was absolutely the worst thing to say to Icky, who immediately stared straight at the dogs and even gave them a little wave.

The dogs did not wave back.

Without the slightest sense of danger, Icky skipped up to the dogs and offered them a high five. "How's it going, boys?" he trilled.

No dog offered its paw, or looked at all likely to.

"We're not boys," rasped a corgi. "We're dogs."

Note from Blue Soup:

After the Spoonheads had sorted out all human problems, they conducted various experiments on animals, including teaching several species how to speak. However, they were forced to leave before these experiments were completed. That was why (for example) dogs could only speak English, which annoyed a lot of children in France, China and some parts of Wales.

"How's it going, dogs?" said
Icky.

Still the dogs viewed
Icky coldly. One or two
ears began to flatten. One
or two lips began to curl.

"Uh-oh," murmured
Stinky.

Suddenly a scraggy little
yorkie leapt forward at Icky,
slavering and snarling. "Want
some?" it yapped. "Want
some, do you?"

"Got some, thanks," said
Icky. He gave the dogs his best winning smile,
except this time it didn't seem to be winning.

The dogs took a step forward.

Icky took a step back.

The dogs took another step forward.

Icky ran like hell.

The dogs just laughed.

"You nearly had it there," said Stinky, as Icky scrambled back to him.

"They were only playing," said Icky.

"I don't think so," said Stinky.

"Anyway," said Icky, "they couldn't hurt me."

"Why not?" asked Stinky.

"Because," said Icky, "I've got my lucky feather."

Stinky wasn't convinced. "You mark my words," he said. "Animals are going to cause big trouble, sooner or later."

Icky wasn't sure exactly how to mark Stinky's words, and in any case, he wasn't one for worrying about bad things till they happened and it was too late to worry.

The two mates walked on, and in time the TV studio came into view. A small boy was running up and down in front of it, punching the air and scoring imaginary goals.

"And Bryan Brain tucks it away," he cried. "And Bryan Brain wins again!"

"I wonder who that is?" mused Stinky.

"I think it might be Bryan Brain," replied Icky.

"What's he playing at?" asked Stinky, who had never in his life punched the air, or – come to that – run.

"It looks like a party," said Icky. "The kind you have when you've got no friends."

Stinky was having second thoughts about teaming up with Bryan Brain, but, as usual, Icky dashed straight in. With a cry of, "Come on, Stinky!" he started leaping around just like Bryan, yelling, "You the man!" and, "There's only one Bryan Brain!"

Bryan Brain, meanwhile, had stopped still. "Who are you?" he asked.

"We're your friends from school!" trilled Icky. "Remember, Bryo?"

"I never remember people," replied Bryan Brain. "I only remember important things, like the distance from Addis Ababa to Timbuctu."

"In that case," said Icky, "we've got just the job for you."

Chapter Two

Stinky, Icky and Bryan Brain gazed in amazement at Uncle Nero's house. It stood like a medieval castle on the top of its own little hill, with daffodils poking through the snow around it. But it didn't actually *look* like a castle, or anything else for that matter. Rooms jutted out all over the place, like strange machines, and no two windows were the same. The front door was huge and strong, and a set of rough stone steps led down from there to a gate. By the gate was a mailbox.

"Right," said Bryan. "I think there should be a vote of thanks to Bryan Brain for finding—"

"Let's see if your uncle's got any mail!" cried Icky.

Icky rushed up to the mailbox, peered through

the slot at the top, then leapt back like he'd been shot. "Woah!" he cried.

"What's up, Icks?" said Stinky.

"There's … something in there!" stammered Icky. "Something … with eyes!"

Stinky put his own eyes to the slot. "Uncle Nero!" he cried. "What are you doing in there?"

A distant, creaky voice replied: *Not much.*

"We came to see if you were still alive," said Stinky.

I knew you were coming, said the voice.

"Wow," said Stinky. "How?"

I've still got a nose, replied the voice.

At this point Bryan piped up. "Having a nose means nothing," he said, "unless the olfactory receptors are working."

There was a pause.

Who's that twit? said the voice.

"Just a friend," said Stinky.

There was another pause.

Could you ask Aunty Vi to get me a nice cup of tea? asked the voice.

This was a difficult moment for Stinky.

Uncle Nero obviously knew nothing about the Spoonheads.

"I'm afraid Aunty Vi's ... gone somewhere," said Stinky. "Somewhere ... different."

"Yeah!" cried Icky. "She's been sucked into a space zoo!"

Icky, as usual, was not very good at telling Little White Lies, or saying The Right Thing.

A space zoo? repeated the voice. *Has she gone to look at wild aliens?*

"More the other way round," said Stinky.

I don't understand, said the voice.

Stinky decided to explain everything. First he explained how a TV programme called !@#! had become the most popular programme in the world ever. It wasn't easy to describe !@#!, except to say it included cookery, extreme sports and attractive people in their bathers, with a rollover jackpot of £30 billion, except you had to watch every programme for five years to win it.

Thanks to !@#!, everything started running down, and no one even noticed when the Spoonheads landed and started making very drastic changes. When they finally did notice, it was too late. Dogs could talk, adults were on their way to the space zoo, and Blue Soup was installed as the operating system for the world. There was little resistance from kids, because they could now stay up as late as they liked. In fact everything was quite good, apart from the fact there was no point in getting up.

If Aunty Vi's gone, said the voice, *who's looking after the house?*

"No one," replied Stinky.

The voice suddenly became urgent.

Stinky! it croaked. *You must do me a great favour. That house is my life's work. You must guard it with your own life!*

A worried frown appeared on Stinky's brow. Stinky did not like responsibility, or any other word with more than ten letters.

"Will you tell me what to do?" he asked nervously.

Sorry, replied the voice. *In ten seconds I go back into*

ultra-slumber for the next fifty years. There's an instruction
book by the phone.

Uncle Nero's last words trailed off slow and deep, like a run-down tape. Stinky was left gaping at the huge house-machine, wondering what on earth he'd let himself in for.

Note from Blue Soup:

I realise this is a very short chapter, but it just seems to have come to an end.

Chapter Three

Icky, Stinky and Bryan Brain puzzled over the instruction book. It was useful having Bryan around, because he could give Stinky handy tips, e.g. always start reading from the top left hand corner of the page (unless, of course, it is in Chinese). However, even with Bryan's handy tips, Stinky couldn't make much sense of the book. As far as Stinky was concerned, it *was* in Chinese.

"There's a map in the back," said Icky. "Let's look at that instead."

Despite Bryan's protests, that was exactly what they did:

Time Travel Garage

The "Undersea World of Uncle Nero"
Bathroom

Outer Space Garden

Attic of Horrors

The Uninvited Guest Bedroom

Cheesy Dreams Bedroom

Dressing (up) Room

Random Madness Gym

Satan's Crypt

Super Safari Viewing Lounge

Kitchen of Magical Invention

Living Living Room

"It sounds *frabjous*," said Icky.

"I'll never look after all that," groaned Stinky.

"Let's explore!" said Icky.

"Hold on," said Bryan Brain. "I agreed to show you the way here. I didn't agree to stay."

"You've got to stay," replied Icky.

"Why?" asked Bryan Brain.

"Because you haven't got a family," replied Icky, "or any friends."

"I have got a friend!" protested Bryan.

"Oh yeah?" challenged Icky. "Who?"

"Jim!" blurted Bryan.

"Jim who?" asked Icky.

"Jim ... Jams!" blurted Bryan.

"Jim Jams?" sneered Icky. "Jim Jams isn't a friend! Jim Jams is what you wear to bed!"

"I don't," said Stinky.

"What do you wear to bed?" asked Icky.

"Trousers, of course," replied Stinky.

"Don't you *ever* take off your trousers?" asked Icky.

"Er ..." said Stinky, "no."

"You must take off your trousers!" protested Bryan. "What about when you go to the toilet?"

"Take off your trousers to go to the toilet?" said Stinky. "Now, there's an idea."

A look of utter horror came over Bryan Brain's face. "You are *disgusting!*" he cried. "Filthy, repulsive, and worse than an animal!"

"Thank you, Bryan," replied Stinky. "Only true friends tell you the truth."

Stinky laid a grubby hand on Bryan's shoulder. A small maggot crept on to Bryan's cardigan, and a shy smile on to his face.

31

"Can we explore now?" asked Icky.

"OK," replied Bryan.

The three great mates set off, all in different directions. They hadn't got far when there was a cry from Icky: "Look what I've found!"

Icky had found the Visitors' Book. Anyone who had ever visited Uncle Nero's house was in there. For example:

NAME	ARRIVED	LEFT	COMMENTS
Arthur Vole	23 Jan	25 Jan	A most agreeable stay.
Daffy Gumshoe	5 Feb	9 Feb	Very nice.
Hilda Grim	2 March	3 March	Thank you, had a pleasant time.
Rolf Piddle	13 Apr	18 Aug	Excellent, apart from getting lost for three months.

All this was quite boring, till Icky turned to the very last page, and found the very last entry:

NAME	ARRIVED	LEFT	COMMENTS
Dronezone	7 Dec		

"Wow!" cried Icky. "Dronezone!"

"Who is Dronezone?" asked Bryan.

"Everyone's heard of Dronezone!" cried Icky. "They're the most popular boy band in the world!"

"I only listen to classical music," replied Bryan.

"Icky," said Stinky, "if they haven't left …"

"… then they're still here!" cried Icky.

"But where?" asked Stinky.

"Let's try … the back garden!" said Icky.

The three great mates set off for the back door. As they were on a mission, Bryan decided there ought to be a leader, and that leader ought to be Bryan. It was Bryan's job to open the door and take the first step outside.

Alas, Bryan had forgotten the golden rule. Always look both ways before crossing the road, or stepping into outer space. There was a forlorn cry as he disappeared down a wormhole into the furthest reaches of the cosmos.

"There you go," said Icky, tapping the map. "Outer Space Garden, just like it says."

Stinky looked into the vast star-studded blackness outside the back door and sighed.

"We'd only just got to know him," he said.

"That's life," said Icky. "Let's check out the living room."

"Hang on a second," said Stinky. There was a rubber ring hanging on the back door, under a sign saying IN CASE OF ACCIDENTAL SPACE MISSION. Stinky took down the ring and flung it rather hopelessly into space. "You never know," he said.

Icky led the way into the living room, but just then there was a knock at the door.

"I'll get it," said Stinky.

Stinky opened the front door. A pig was standing outside. "I want a pork pie," it said.

Stinky rubbed his eyes and looked again. Things were just getting too weird. "You can't say that!" he protested.

"Why not?" said the pig.

"You've got to say 'please', or something," said Stinky.

"Please or something," said the pig. "Now give me a pork pie."

"No!" cried Stinky.

"Why not?" snarled the pig.

34

"You're a pig!" cried Stinky. "You can't eat pork pies! That would be like me eating a … a person pie!"

The pig licked his lips. "Mmm," he said. "Person pie. That does sound inviting."

"Goodbye," said Stinky, shutting the door.

There was an angry knock, then another, and finally the sound of furious trotters stamping away.

"I knew animals were going to cause trouble," said Stinky. Just then he heard a cry for help from Icky. He hurried to the living room, where he found his great mate trapped in an armchair. Somehow the arms of a chair had wrapped themselves around Icky, and were now holding him fast.

"I just sat down," gasped Icky, "and it started cuddling me."

"Maybe it likes you," said Stinky.

"Get it off!" cried Icky.

Using most of his strength, and all of his smell, Stinky persuaded the armchair to let go.

Icky jumped up, eyes darting around nervously.

"The room's alive!" he cried. "It really is a Living Living Room!"

Stinky looked around. Everything seemed fairly normal and average and ordinary, except for the four potatoes on the sofa. In front of these potatoes was a very impressive telly. Stinky was quite surprised about this, because Uncle Nero had always hated TV.

"I wonder if the telly works?" he mused, switching it on.

A giant eye appeared on the screen.

"I don't think I know this programme," said Stinky.

Stinky walked over to the left.

The eye moved to the left.

Stinky walked over to the right.

The eye moved to the right.

"Icky," said Stinky, "I think the telly is watching us."

"That's nothing," said Icky, "I think the potatoes are talking."

Stinky listened very closely. Sure enough, there was a tiny tinny sound coming from the direction of the potatoes. Icky put his ear right next to them. A look of surprise came over his face. He nodded, and nodded again, and said "A-ha" three times.

"What are they saying?" asked Stinky.

"They're telling us not to look at the telly," replied Icky. "If we watch it for more than thirty seconds, we'll turn into potatoes like them."

"So they haven't always been potatoes?" said Stinky.

"No," said Icky. "They used to be Dronezone."

"Ah!" said Stinky, "that's where they got to!"

"On the other hand," said Icky, "they might be lying."

"That's true," said Stinky. "They might be another boy band."

"We could get them to sing something," suggested Icky.

"No, don't bother," said Stinky.

Icky yawned. "Now that we've found Dronezone," he said, "I suggest we turn in."

"OK," said Stinky. He turned off the telly and the two great mates headed for the bedrooms. But just as they passed the back door, Stinky remembered Bryan, and began to feel very sorry.

"He may still come back," said Icky. "Our cat went missing for five days, but he turned up in the end."

"You've just given me an idea," said Stinky.

Note from Blue Soup:
Stinky had at least one idea every year, usually around Christmas.

Stinky went into the kitchen and came back with a spoon and a bowl. He opened the back door, and tap-tap-tapped the bowl with the spoon.

"Bry-an!" he called. "Here, Bry-bry-bry-bry-bryan!"

There was a little cry out in the darkness, then Bryan came hurtling towards them, wearing the rubber ring that Stinky had thrown out earlier.

"Bryan!" said Stinky. "Where have you been?"

"Don't ask," said Bryan.

His hair was full of bits of rock, and there was a small piece of satellite in his pocket.

"We found Dronezone," said Icky.

"And a pig came to the door," added Stinky.

"Did it?" asked Icky.

"Yes, I was going to tell you," said Stinky. "It wanted a pork pie."

"I hope you gave him one," said Bryan.

"No," said Stinky. "Why?"

"Don't you read the news?" asked Bryan.

"No," said Stinky, "Why?"

Suddenly there was a huge crash at the front door. The three great mates rushed to the window. A gang of pigs were at the gate. Beside them was a giant catapult.

"Well done, Stinky," said Bryan. "Now we're at war."

Chapter Four

Note from Blue Soup:

We now carry on from exactly where we left off.

"W-what do you think they're going to do?" asked Stinky, nervously.

"Well," said Bryan, "I suppose they're going to lay siege to us till we surrender."

"I don't like the sound of that," said Icky.

"Whatever it means," added Stinky.

The three great mates watched the pigs busily going about their business. They were loading something on to the catapult.

"I wonder what that is," said Stinky.

Bryan stroked his chin, like a professor. "In the Middle Ages," he said, "they would sometimes fling a dead body over the town walls, to spread horrible diseases."

"Maybe they'll do that!" said Icky.

All the colour drained out of Stinky's face. "Let's go to the kitchen," he said, "and get a pork pie."

Icky, Stinky and Bryan Brain went to the kitchen. The kitchen looked fairly normal, apart from one thing: there wasn't any food. Nothing in the fridge, nothing in the cupboards, and nothing on the shelves.

"Now what are we going to do?" said Stinky.

"We could give them a baked potato," suggested Icky.

"There aren't any potatoes," said Stinky.

"Oh yes, there are," replied Icky.

Stinky, as usual, took a while to catch on. "We can't bake Dronezone!" he cried.

"Stinky," said Icky, "you promised your uncle you would defend his house with your life!"

"Yes," said Stinky, "not with Dronezone's life!"

But help was at hand. Bryan had discovered a book inside the washing machine. The book was called *101 Great Spells to Make Your Dinner Party Go With a Bang*.

"It appears," he said, "that we can make food with spells."

"Wicked!" said Icky, forgetting all about baking the world's favourite boy band.

Bryan was a person who knew about books, so he turned straight to the back pages, found the INDEX, and looked up PORK PIES.

"A-ha," he said. "Spell for pork pies, page 365."

Bryan looked up the spell. His face dropped. "*What?*" he said. "*What?*" he said again.

"What?" asked Stinky.

"We've got to put an empty tray in the Oven Of Sorcery," said Bryan.

"What's the problem with that?" asked Icky.

"Then, we've got to say the magic spell," added Bryan. "The magic spell from the magic pantomime."

"What magic pantomime?" asked Stinky.

"Snow White and the Seven Panto Horses," replied Bryan.

"What's wrong with that?" asked Icky.

"We've got to do it *in costume*," replied Bryan.

"Brilliant!" said Icky. "I love dressing up."

"I don't," grumbled Bryan, "and I'm not going to do it."

43

At this point there was another almighty CRASH at the front door. The whole house seemed to shake. So did Bryan.

"We'd better find the dressing room," said Icky.

Icky and Stinky headed upstairs. Bryan followed meekly. They opened the door marked DRESSING (UP) ROOM, and gasped. The room inside was jam-packed with clothes racks, shoe racks, and hat racks. There were Roman costumes, costumes from old Japan, cowboy costumes and caveman outfits. Icky's eyes bulged, and Bryan's lip trembled.

"Bags I be the front end of the horse!" said Stinky, who'd spotted the costume.

"I'm not being Snow White!" cried Icky.

"OK," said Stinky. "You be the back end of the horse."

"I'll be Snow White," said Icky.

Icky and Stinky grabbed the costumes and hurried back downstairs. Bryan dragged his heels after them. By the time he reached the kitchen, Icky was already Snow White, and Stinky was already the front end of the horse.

"Come on, Bryan," said Icky, "get the back legs on, get in behind Stinky, and I'll zip the two halves together."

Bryan pulled on the back legs ever-so-slowly. The thought of being zipped in behind Stinky terrified him. "I don't think I can do this," he said.

Icky decided to take charge of the situation. He laid a fatherly hand on Bryan's shoulder.

"There comes a moment in every boy's life," he said, "when that boy must become a man."

Bryan's lip stopped trembling.

"This is your moment, Bryan," said Icky.

Bryan took a deep, deep breath. He seemed to stand six inches taller. "Zip me in, Icky," he pronounced.

"Good man," said Icky.

Bryan got up behind Stinky, and Icky began to zip the two halves of the Panto Horse together.

"Hold it a moment!" said Bryan. "Stinky – you promise you won't do a ... you know."

"What?" said Stinky.

"You know," said Bryan.

"What?" said Stinky.

"I can't say it," said Bryan.

"Why not?" said Stinky.

"Because," said Bryan, "it's the rudest word in the world."

"If you don't say it," said Stinky, "how can I promise not to do it?"

"For Pete's sake!" cried Icky. "Just say it, Bryan!"

"Parpy," mumbled Bryan.

There was a short silence.

"Parpy?" said Icky. "*Parpy* is the rudest word in the world?"

"Stop saying it!" cried Bryan.

"All right, all right," said Stinky. "I promise not to do it, Bryan."

"Cross your heart and hope to die?" said Bryan.

"I can't cross my heart," replied Stinky. "I've got hooves on my hands."

"Swear on your mother's life, then," said Bryan.

"My mother's in the space zoo," replied Stinky.

"Swear on the most precious thing you know, then!" said Bryan.

"OK," said Stinky. "I swear on Norman, my pet flea."

Bryan took another deep breath. "OK, Icky," he said. "Zip me in."

Icky zipped the Panto Horse tight shut.

"Now, listen very carefully, Icky," said Bryan, in a muffled, serious voice. "Do not touch that zip again until we've got the pie. Is that clear?"

"Right on, captain," said Icky.

"Proceed," said Bryan.

"Yes," said Stinky. "Do whatever he said."

Icky checked the spell book. "OK, lads," he said. "Let's learn the dance moves first. One, two, kick to the right … one, two, kick to the left."

Snow White and the Panto Horse practised the dance moves.

"Good," said Icky. He placed a tray in the oven, shut the oven door, and pressed the On button. "Now we sing 'Horsey, Horsey', while doing the dance."

Snow White and the Panto Horse began to dance and sing at the same time:

"Horsey, horsey, don't you stop!

Just let your heels go clippety-clop!

Your tail goes swish, your wheels go round!

Giddy-up, we're—"

"Stop! Stop!" cried Stinky.

They all stopped.

"I'm very sorry," said Stinky, "but I'm about to break my promise."

"*What?*" cried Bryan.

"It's all the jigging about," said Stinky.

There was a short pause, then the back end of the horse went berserk. "Get me out of here!" it screeched.

"We haven't got the pie yet," said Icky.

"I'm going to die!" bawled Bryan. He cursed and yelled and kicked and punched. Icky folded his arms. "You told me not to touch the zip," he said.

"I never meant it!" screamed Bryan.

"Not until we've got the pie, you said," said Icky.

"Hang the stupid pie!" bawled Bryan.

Suddenly there was a loud bang and a flash of light. The oven door fell open to reveal a huge, glistening pork pie, which didn't look stupid at all.

"It worked!" cried Icky. He calmly unzipped the horse. Bryan staggered out, coughing, spluttering and cursing. At the sight of the giant pie, however, his awful experience was suddenly forgotten. "Wow," he said.

"If that doesn't end the war," said Stinky, "nothing will."

Everyone climbed out of their costumes. Icky lifted the pie out of the oven and on to a big blue plate. Stinky carried the plate to the front door.

"Shouldn't we hold up a white flag?" asked Bryan.

"That's an idea," said Icky. "Have we got anything white?"

"My undies are white," said Stinky. "At least, they were the last time I saw them."

"Let's forget the white flag," said Bryan.

"We'll just open the door and shout 'Hold your fire!'" said Icky.

The three mates did just that. It was a dramatic moment. The pigs stopped loading the catapult, and one of them stepped forward. He wore a general's hat and a patch over one eye. "Well, looky here," he said.

Note from Blue Soup:
General Pig spoke with the accent of the Deep South of the USA. Actually, he'd never been to America, but he had seen a lot of films (before the Spoonheads filled the cinemas with glue).

"We bring the Pie Of Peace," said Icky.

General Pig turned to his army. "Keep me covered, boys," he said. He crunched through the dirty snow to the top of the steps and took a good close look at the pie. "What kind of pie is this?" he asked.

"It's a pork pie," said Stinky. "You know, the kind pigs like."

"Don't you tell me what pigs like, boy!" snapped General Pig.

"But the other pig—" began Stinky.

"Don't want no pork pie, boy!" snapped General
Pig.

General Pig's words echoed off the walls. Bryan
really wanted to tell the general that he should
have said "*any* pork pie", but even Bryan wasn't that
stupid.

"What kind of pie do you want?" asked Stinky
nervously.

General Pig leaned closer, right up to Stinky's

face. General Pig really was ugly close up, with one very mean thin eye, and a snout full of wrinkles and mud.

"The pie we want," he sneered, "is a person pie."

Everything went silent.

"Ain't that right, pigs?" cried the general.

The pigs cheered loudly and rattled their knives and forks.

"Well, tough!" said Icky. "Cos you got a pork pie!"

Icky flung the pie straight into the general's face and sprinted back indoors. Needless to say, the general was quite surprised. So, for that matter, were Stinky and Bryan. Then they came to their senses, raced after Icky, and slammed the door shut.

"What did you do that for?" squealed Bryan, panting for breath.

"Didn't like him," said Icky.

"We're for it now!" groaned Stinky.

Sure enough, General Pig was stamping down the steps, angrily sweeping crumbs from his snout. "Let 'em have it!" he cried. The pigs loaded the catapult, and next second there was the most almighty crash.

"Whatever that was," said Bryan, "it's come through!"

"But where?" asked Stinky.

"It sounded like upstairs," said Icky.

The three great mates hurried upstairs and explored all the rooms. They found a lot of unusual things, but they did not find the whatever-it-was.

"There's only one place we haven't searched," said Bryan.

"The Attic of Horrors," said Icky.

Chapter Five

Icky, Stinky and Bryan looked up at the dark attic hatch, and shuddered.

"Maybe we should just forget about it," said Stinky.

"We can't do that," said Icky. "The pigs might have catapulted in a bomb."

"Or a dead body with a horrible disease," added Bryan.

There was no way round it. Someone had to get up in that attic.

"I vote for Bryan," said Stinky.

"Why me?" said Bryan.

"Look at it this way," said Icky. "You've fallen down a black hole and been in a panto horse with Stinky. What worse thing can happen to you?"

"All right," said Bryan. "I'll go first, but you two can follow."

Bryan pushed open the hatch. There was a blast of cold fusty air.

"What can you see?" asked Stinky.

"Nothing," said Bryan. "It's pitch black."

"Try feeling around," said Icky. "There might be a light switch."

Bryan began feeling around in the darkness. A horrible sense of doom was coming over him. Bryan had a terrible fear of spiders, and he was sure a spider was about to run over his hand. At first, however, all he could feel was dust and wooden floorboards. Then, suddenly, he came on something which sent a shiver through his liver.

"It's all sticky!" he cried.

"What is it?" asked Icky.

"Some kind of rope," said Bryan.

"Can you see it?" asked Stinky.

"My eyes haven't adjusted to the dark," replied Bryan.

"I see," said Stinky, who didn't.

"Maybe it's a spider thread!" said Icky.

"Don't be stupid!" said Bryan, in a sudden panic. "To make thread that thick, a spider would have to be five metres wide!"

"Wow," said Icky. "Imagine that!"

"Can you see yet?" asked Stinky.

Bryan peered into the gloom. "I'm starting to see something," he said.

"What is it?" asked Stinky.

"I'm not sure," said Bryan, "but it's—"

Bryan stopped short. A strangled wobbly noise came from his throat.

"It's what?" asked Stinky.

"It's … about five metres wide," warbled Bryan.

"Hmm," said Icky. "Has it got a lot of legs?"

"E-eight," stammered Bryan.

"I always thought spiders had six legs," said Icky.

"Well, you're stupid!" said Bryan. "*Insects* have got six legs, not spiders!"

"Aren't spiders insects?" asked Icky.

"No, you idiot!" cried Bryan. "They're *arachnids*!"

"No need to get stroppy," said Icky.

"I've got every reason to get stroppy!" said Bryan. "There's a five-metre spider in front of me!"

"Is it alive?" asked Stinky.

"It's staring right at me!" cried Bryan. "With six eyes!"

"I always thought spiders had two eyes," said Icky.

"Just shut up!" screamed Bryan.

Stinky decided to try to calm things down. "It's all right, Bryan," he said. "You've got your mates right behind you."

"I'd rather have them in front of me," said Bryan.

"Can you see the thing the pigs threw?" asked Stinky.

"I can ... see ... a hole," replied Bryan shakily. "A hole ... in the roof."

"Then it's there somewhere," said Stinky.

"Yes!" said Bryan. "I can see something … something like a bomb."

"Oh good," said Icky. "Then it's not a dead body with a horrible disease."

"Where is the bomb, Bryan?" asked Stinky.

"It's … right in front of the spider," replied Bryan.

"OK, Bryan," said Stinky. "I've got a plan."

"What is it?" asked Bryan.

"You go and get the bomb," said Stinky.

Bryan spluttered. "That's not a plan!" he cried. "That's a suicide mission!"

"It can't hurt you," said Icky.

"Can't hurt me?" gasped Bryan. "Don't you know what spiders *do*? They seize their prey in a death lock, inject them with poison that turns their insides to goo, then drink them for dinner!"

There was a short silence.

"Bryan," said Icky, "there comes a moment in every boy's life when that boy must become a man."

Bryan pondered. "Haven't I heard that before?" he asked.

"Just grab the bomb," said Stinky. "Otherwise it's Certain Death for all of us."

Bryan clambered up into the attic, heart pounding like a jack-hammer.

The spider stayed very still.

Bryan crept forward.

Six shiny black eyes stared at Bryan, as cold as metal. But the spider made no move.

Bryan got a bit more confident. A couple more steps …

… one more …

Suddenly Icky and Stinky heard a shriek. "It's got me!"

Stinky shook his head. "Poor Bryan," he said. "It's really not his day."

"Help me!" screamed Bryan. "For pity's sake, help me!"

Icky scrambled into the attic and ran in the direction of Bryan's screams. "I'll get you, spider!" he bawled.

But Icky was in for a surprise. There was no spider. Bryan was totally alone.

"Bryan," said Icky, "you're struggling against nothing."

"What are you talking about?" gasped Bryan. "It's got me!"

Bryan twisted frantically this way and that, as if fighting to get himself free. Icky watched him open-mouthed. Then he noticed the ticking.

The bomb!

Icky looked down. There, sure enough, was a deadly grey box, just a metre away. On the top was a timer, which at that second said 2.04.

"Two hours," said Icky. "That's not too bad."

"That's not two hours!" cried Bryan. "That's two minutes!"

Icky went into a flat panic. He grabbed for the bomb, but his hand stopped short.

Icky had seen something.

Something deadly.

Right behind the bomb, nestling in the shadows, was the sinister coiled body of a lethal king cobra. Before Icky's horrified eyes, it slowly unwound, then reared up, neck swelling, fangs poised to strike. Icky began to back away, and as he did so, felt a tap on his shoulder.

"Stinky?" he murmured.

Icky glanced back – just in time to see a massive python slithering down from the rafters to wrap itself around him in a monster squeeze of death.

"Help!" cried Icky. "It's got me!"

"What's got you?" gasped Bryan.

"The snake!" cried Icky.

"What snake?" asked Bryan.

"This snake!" cried Icky. "Can't you see it?"

"No," said Bryan. "Can't you see the spider?"

Something clicked in Icky's brain. "Hold on," he said. "If I can't see the spider, and you can't see the snake, can't you see what's happening?"

"I'm having my innards turned to goo!" wailed Bryan.

"No, you're not!" cried Icky. "You're just seeing what you're scared of! And I'm seeing what *I'm* scared of! That must be how this attic works!"

"But it's real!" cried Bryan.

"You just *think* it's real!" cried Icky.

61

Bryan tried to take this in, then remembered what they were there for. "Get the bomb then!" he cried.

"I can't!" cried Icky.

"Why not?" cried Bryan.

"The python's got me!" cried Icky.

Icky looked at Bryan. Bryan looked at Icky. "Stinky!" they cried.

Stinky's head appeared through the hatch.

"Stinky!" cried Icky. "The bomb's there, see? Grab it and sling it out of a window!"

"OK," said Stinky.

Stinky lazily dragged himself up into the attic and began shambling towards the bomb.

Stinky wasn't afraid of spiders or snakes and therefore couldn't see either. "What's the matter with you two?" he asked.

"Never mind," said Icky.

Stinky reached for the bomb. But just at that moment, his eyes opened wide. "No!" he cried. "No, not that!"

"What is it, Stinky?" asked Icky.

"It's ... soap!" cried Stinky. "A massive, monster bar of soap!"

"Ignore it, Stinky!" cried Icky. "It's not really there!"

"It's coming for me!" cried Stinky.

"Just grab the bomb and leg it!" cried Icky.

The awful perfume was almost too much for Stinky to bear, but he summoned up every ounce of courage, grabbed the bomb, and legged it.

Ten seconds left.

Stinky vanished back through the hatch. That seemed to break the spell for Bryan and Icky. They fought free of the python and the spider, and raced after Stinky.

"Out the window, Stinky!" cried Icky.

Bryan and Icky stared down through the hatch. Stinky was sitting on the floor, quite calm, quietly studying the bomb.

"Stinky, you goon!" cried Icky. "Fling it!"

Icky and Bryan ducked for cover, put their hands over their ears, and prayed.

Nothing happened.

Icky and Bryan peered nervously down.

Stinky was holding the bomb at arm's length. Slowly he turned it towards Icky. The timer had disappeared. In fact, it wasn't a bomb at all. It was a block of ice.

"But ..." stammered Bryan.

"*I see what's happened!*" said Icky.

Icky explained what had happened to Bryan, who was very clever in some ways, and quite amazingly stupid in others.

Note from Blue Soup:

I'm sure you're not as slow as Bryan, so I won't bother pointing out that all three of them were afraid of bombs.

"All that for nothing!" sighed Bryan.

Suddenly there was another massive smash. The pigs had hit the roof again.

"The house can't take much more of this," said Stinky.

"What can we do?" asked Bryan.

"There's only one thing we *can* do," said Icky.

"I agree," said Stinky. "What's that then?"

"Give them a person pie," replied Icky.

Chapter Six

Icky, Stinky and Bryan Brain sat in the kitchen. An empty red chair was in front of them.

"Right," said Icky. "Who's first?"

"I'll go first," said Bryan.

Bryan took a seat in the red chair. He propped his chin on his thumb and looked very thoughtful.

"Bryan Brain," said Icky. "You now have two minutes to persuade us why you should not go in the person pie."

"I understand," said Bryan.

"Begin," said Icky.

"I am the cleverest person left alive," said Bryan. "The human race needs me."

"Hmm," said Icky. "Where do you see yourself in ten years?"

"Prime Minister," replied Bryan.

"Ha!" said Icky. "There *is* no prime minister, cos everything's run by Blue Soup!"

"I'm cleverer than Blue Soup," said Bryan.

"Are not!" said Icky.

"Am!" said Bryan.

"This is getting us nowhere," said Stinky. "What do you taste like, Bryan?"

"Salty and stringy," said Bryan. "Not very nice at all."

"How do you know?" snapped Icky.

"I ate a blister," replied Bryan.

"Eurrr," said Stinky.

"You definitely don't deserve to survive," said Icky.

"Can I get down now?" said Bryan.

Next it was Icky's turn. He grinned and hugged his knees as if all this was a great laugh.

"Icky Bats," said Stinky, "you now have two minutes to persuade us why you should not go in the person pie."

"I am the bravest," said Icky, "the best-looking, the funniest, and the most modest. Also, I've got a lucky feather."

"And where do you see yourself in ten years?" asked Bryan.

"Not in a pig's stomach," said Icky. "Your turn, Stinky."

Icky hopped up. Stinky took his place. He flopped back like a sack of potatoes and scratched his head. "What am I supposed to say?" he asked.

"You're supposed to tell us," said Bryan, "why you deserve to survive."

Stinky looked gormlessly back at Bryan.

"The answer's not written on my face!" said Bryan. It was something he'd once heard a teacher say.

Stinky ummed and erred and puzzled and puzzled. Finally he gave up. "Nope," he said. "Can't think of a reason."

Bryan sighed. "Do we need to bother with a vote?" he asked.

"Yes!" said Icky. "We do!" Icky had decided to disagree with Bryan, whatever he said.

Bryan sighed again. "Very well," he said. He handed Stinky and Icky a pen and paper each, and took one for himself.

"Does anyone have any last words to say?" asked Stinky.

"May the best man win," said Bryan, "which is me."

"What about you, Icky?" said Stinky. "Any last words?"

"Yes," said Icky. "Here's ten pounds, Stinky."

Icky handed Stinky a tenner.

"You can't do that!" cried Bryan.

"Why not?" asked Icky.

"That's a bribe!" cried Bryan.

"Who said we couldn't bribe?" asked Icky.

Bryan went red with fury. "Right!" he snapped. "Here's *twenty* pounds, Stinky!" He handed Stinky two tenners, then presented a big smarmy smile to Icky.

"Thank you, Bryan," said Stinky. "Shall we vote now?"

The three great mates cast their votes, then put them into a little green pot. Bryan took them out again, one by one, in a very solemn way.

"One vote for Stinky," said Bryan, but his smile didn't last long. "One vote for Bryan," he mumbled.

So. The final vote was crucial.

Bryan took out the third vote. He didn't seem to want to read it.

"What's it say, Bryan?" asked Icky.

Bryan's lip trembled. "Why did you both vote for me?" he snivelled.

"To be honest, Bryan," said Stinky, "it was because you tried to bribe me."

"But Icky bribed you first!" moaned Bryan.

"Icky only gave me a tenner," said Stinky. "You gave me twenty."

"I voted for you because you ate a blister," said Icky.

Bryan was lost for words.

"So, Bryan," said Icky, "how are we going to do this?" He began leafing through *101 Great Spells To Make Your Dinner Party Go With a Bang.* "I think we should cook the pastry first," he said, "then you should climb in."

Bryan began to cry. "Why does everything bad happen to me?" he sobbed.

Stinky watched Bryan crying, and remembered how sad he had been when Bryan got lost in space. "Icky," he said, "I know Bryan lost the vote, but I really don't think I can cook him in a pie."

"What's the choice?" said Icky.

"Maybe we could *pretend* he's in the pie," suggested Stinky.

"Yes!" cried Bryan. "Maybe we could make a chicken pie, then *say* it's a person pie."

"Why should the pigs believe us?" asked Icky.

"We'll put my cap on top of the pie!" said Bryan.

Icky thought about this. "It's worth a shot," he said.

"Yes!" cried Bryan.

Icky flicked through the spell book. "Chicken pie ..." he muttered. "Ah! Chicken pie."

"It doesn't involve panto horses, does it?" asked Bryan.

"No," said Icky. "Something much worse than that."

Bryan seized the recipe book. As his eyes scanned the lines, all the colour drained out of his face. "Oh no!" he groaned. "Not *that*!"

Chapter Seven

Icky, Stinky and Bryan looked down at the chicken pie and breathed a sigh of relief. Bryan placed his cap on top of it and wiped the last of the revolting purple goo from his face.

"Thank heaven that's over," said Icky. "Let's go face the pigs."

Note from Blue Soup:

I realise some of you might like to know how the great mates made the chicken pie. However, the Spoonheads laid down certain rules for stories which I must follow. Rule 89 has caused a lot of argument, so I will quote it in full:

'89. Every story must contain at least one passage where the reader has to think for themselves.'

It may seem hard, but the Spoonheads wanted to see lively-minded, imaginative children, not dull sponges who soak up everything that is thrown at them.

Anyway, the spell was far too disgusting to put in a book, even a book for children.

Icky and Stinky faced the pigs alone. That seemed sensible. If Bryan was with them, the pigs might guess he wasn't in the pie.

"Person pie," said Icky. "Come and get it."

General Pig raised his arm. "OK, pigs," he said. "Hold your fire."

General Pig drew a napkin slowly from his pocket, shook it out, and tied it around his neck. Then he pulled a knife and fork from the other pocket and click-clacked up the steps, whistling. Stinky hopefully offered the pie up to him.

General Pig drew a deep breath. "Smells pretty good," he said.

"It's Bryan," said Stinky. "He always did smell better than me."

General Pig plucked Bryan's cap from the top of the pie, gave a little snort, and flung it aside.

Then he cut deep into the pie, dug out a huge forkful, and stuffed it into his big dribbling gob.

"Tastes mighty good," said General Pig.

"Thank you," said Stinky.

"Kinda like chicken," said General Pig.

"Really?" said Stinky.

"Bryan said he might taste like chicken," said Icky. "He used to eat a lot of eggs."

Suddenly General Pig stopped eating. He screwed up his one eye and looked into the pie. Then he poked his trotter in and pulled out a wishbone. "What is this?" he asked.

"Er ..." said Icky.

"Er ..." said Stinky.

"Looks like a wishbone," said the general. "A chicken's wishbone."

"Or tweezers," said Icky.

"What?" said General Pig.

"Bryan kept tweezers in his pocket," said Icky, "for his nose hairs."

General Pig looked Icky hard in the eye. "Tweezers made of bone?" he said. "Do you take me for a fool, boy?"

"No," said Icky. "Just a pig."

With that, Icky stuck the rest of the pie over General Pig's head and hared back inside the house, dragging Stinky behind him.

"How did it go?" asked Bryan.

There was a massive smash and the sound of splintering furniture. Stinky shrugged. Bryan groaned. "*Now* what are we going to do?" he pleaded.

"There's only one thing we can do," said Icky. "Fight."

Chapter Eight

The three great mates held a council of war around the kitchen table.

"I've got a lucky feather," said Icky.

"What use is that?" scoffed Bryan.

"Uncle Jav said it would save my life one day," said Icky.

"OK," said Bryan. "You go and attack the pigs with your feather. Then we'll find out if it works."

Icky jumped to his feet. Stinky pressed him gently back down. "Don't worry about the feather. I've got some dirty hankies," he suggested.

"For Pete's sake!" cried Bryan. "What good are dirty hankies?"

"They've gone really hard," said Stinky. "If

they hit you on the head, they'd probably
knock you out."

"Stinky," said Bryan, "they've got a *siege catapult*.
We're not going to beat a *siege catapult* with dirty
hankies."

Bryan was right. The great mates needed a
weapon. A big weapon.

"There must be *something* in this house," said
Bryan. He opened out the map in the instruction
book.

"What about the Time Travel Garage?"
suggested Stinky.

"That's it!" cried Icky. "We'll go to the future, then we'll get a *wicked* weapon!"

Icky, Stinky and Bryan made their way to the garage. This was on the other side of the living room, through a steel door. It was a very well-organised garage, with shelves full of red tin boxes marked SCREWS, HOOKS, TWIDDLY BITS and so on. At the centre of it was a white van, with stacks of bricks instead of wheels. On the side of the van was painted:

A1 REMOVALS

NO JOB TOO SMALL

"I thought there would be a time machine in here," said Icky.

"Maybe that *is* the time machine," said Stinky.

"That?" scoffed Bryan. "Never!"

The three great mates climbed up on to the front seat of the van. It smelled of oil and cold metal, and there were old toffee wrappers and rags everywhere.

"Still think it's a time machine?" asked Bryan.

There was a key in the ignition. "Let's see what happens when we turn this," said Icky.

Icky turned the key. There was a whirr, and a hum, then the whole dashboard began to turn itself inside out. In its place came the most amazing control panel, lit by a thousand coloured lights. A huge list of instructions came down from the rear-view mirror. Metal shields slid up over all the windows and the whole van seemed to throb.

"I'm still not convinced," said Bryan.

"In that case," said Icky, "you can stay here and look after the house."

Bryan suddenly changed his tune. "You can't leave me behind!" he said. "You need me to read all the instructions."

"Oh, we'll manage without instructions," said Stinky.

Bryan left the van with a sulky frown. Icky and Stinky waited for the slam of the garage door, then cast their eyes over the massive dashboard. In the middle of it was a list of dates and a slider control.

"Let's set it for the year 3000," said Icky. "They're bound to have some good weapons in the year 3000."

Stinky pushed the slider up to 3000. "What now?" he asked.

"Suppose we just press that big green button," said Icky.

"Hmm," said Stinky. "Maybe we *should* read the instructions first."

"Nah," said Icky. "Let's just press it."

Icky walloped the button, like a ping-pong player smashing a winner. Suddenly everything seemed to change, but it was difficult to say how. Then Icky turned to Stinky, and had the fright of his life.

Lines were growing over Stinky's face.

Bags were appearing under his eyes.

His hair was turning grey.

His teeth were starting to rot.

"Stinky!" cried Icky. "You're growing old!"

"So are you!" cried Stinky.

Icky felt his face. The skin was all squashy and droopy, like an old flannel. "Quick!" he cried. "Stop the machine!"

There was a red button on Stinky's side of the van. Stinky pressed it. The noises stopped.

"Phew," said Stinky. "That was a close shave."

There was only one problem. Stinky and Icky still looked about ninety. Stinky's back ached, and Icky couldn't remember Stinky's name.

"I think we should get Bryan," said Stinky, in a weak old croaky voice.

Stinky and Icky struggled out of the van. Stinky found a stick to lean on, and Icky found Stinky to lean on. They shuffled out of the garage, through the living room and down the hall. Bryan was in the kitchen, fixing a frying-pan to the end of a broom-handle. At the sight of Icky and Stinky, the whole lot dropped out of his hands.

"Who are you?" he blurted.

"Don't panic," croaked Stinky, "but it's your old mates."

Bryan looked again. "Icky and Stinky?" he murmured.

"Can you help us read the instructions, Bryan?" asked Stinky.

Suddenly Bryan began to laugh. Just a little at first, then louder and louder, till it seemed he might bust a gut.

"Please, Bryan," pleaded Stinky.

"OK," said Bryan, "but first you must say, 'Bryan Brain is our hero and we will never again vote to put him in a pie'."

"Bryan Brain is our hero," said Icky and Stinky, "and we will never again vote to put him in a pie."

"Good," said Bryan. "Now you must say, 'Please come into the future with us, Bryan'."

"Please come into the future with us, Bryan," said Icky and Stinky.

"No, thank you," said Bryan. "I'm too busy."

Bryan swaggered past Icky and Stinky, leading the way back to the garage. Icky and Stinky shuffled slowly along behind. They all struggled up into the van and Bryan read through the instructions, stroking his chin in the usual way.

"Did you fasten your seat belts?" he asked.

"Er," said Stinky, "no."

Tut-tut-tut, went Bryan. "Now you know why you're ninety," he said.

"Can we go back young?" asked Stinky, wiping Icky's dribble off his shoulder.

"You'll have to put the van into reverse," said Bryan.

"OK," said Stinky. "How do we do that, then?"

"With the gearstick," said Bryan.

"Right-o," said Stinky. "Which stick is that, then?"

Note from Blue Soup:

As you've probably noticed, this conversation is about to get very long and tiresome. I shall therefore ignore the rest of it and skip straight to Icky and Stinky's journey to the year 3000. This journey is also quite long and tiresome.

"Are we there yet?" asked Icky.

"Not yet," said Stinky. "Do a wordsearch or something."

"OK," said Icky. He picked up a wordsearch then put it down again. "Are we there yet?" he asked.

"Icky," said Stinky, "you've been asking me that every ten seconds for the last five hundred years."

"Sorry," said Icky. "Are we there yet?"

An orange light began to flash on the dashboard. All the hums and rattles suddenly got louder, then faded to silence. The metal screens came down, and a pleasant sunlight filtered into the time van.

"Hmm," said Stinky. "I think we're there."

Stinky and Icky took off their seatbelts and climbed out of the van. It was parked on top of a mound, but there was no sign of Uncle Nero's house. They were smack in the middle of the most fantastic city they had ever seen, with forests and water and lights mingling with buildings which seemed to be made out of air.

"I wonder where we can get a burger?" said Stinky.

Stinky and Icky set off down the road. They hadn't gone far when a boy came along, about their age. The moment he saw Icky and Stinky, he broke into a wide smile and offered his hand. "How's it going?" he said.

"All right," said Stinky. "Do we know you?"

The boy laughed. "See you at the party," he said, and carried on his way.

"Funny bloke," said Icky.

Stinky stopped. There were a gang of dogs hanging around at the street corner ahead.

"Avoid their eyes," said Stinky.

Too late. A beagle had separated from the pack and was approaching fast.

"How's it going?" said the beagle, offering its paw.

"Er ... fine, thanks," said Stinky.

The beagle put its front legs around Stinky and hugged him. "I love you," it said.

"Steady on," said Stinky.

Soon Icky and Stinky were surrounded by dogs, all wanting to hug them and tell them how much they loved them.

"Are we famous or something?" said Icky.

"See you at the party," said the dogs, moving on.

"This place is *weird*," said Stinky.

Icky and Stinky pressed on. They were looking for a sign saying SHOPS, or MINISTRY OF WAR, but every sign they saw said

PARTY ———>

"This is getting ridiculous," said Stinky.

At last Icky and Stinky arrived at a station. They knew it was a station because it said STATION, and it was full of people hurrying about and climbing into sofa-sized bubbles which skimmed off in every direction. The bubbles were all different colours, and the same colours were shown on a big screen.

BLUE LINE it said, SHOPPING CENTRE.

"That's the one for us," said Icky.

Icky and Stinky climbed into a blue bubble. The moment they closed the door, the bubble set off at fantastic speed, swooping through the city like a giant gull.

"Woah!" said Stinky.

"This is better than the fair!" said Icky.

Fantastic sights swept past them – glass

factories, flats like
holes in the sky,
a field full of
people buzzing
like midges. Then
the bubble slid
silently to a halt at
a sign saying:

SHOP TILL
YOU DROP STOP.

The two great mates climbed out and stared
in amazement. They were in the centre of an
incredible square, surrounded by buildings of every
shape and size, like giant toys. Every shop had an
exciting name, like PINK ROBOTS R US, GOING
SPACE PLACES, and YE OLDE 29th CENTURY
BYGONE SHOP.

"I hope they take Blue Soup cards," said Stinky.

"We don't need them," said Icky. "Can't you see
the posters?"

Stinky looked again at the shop windows:

TAKE WHAT YOU LIKE
EVERYTHING MUST GO

"Frabjous!" said Stinky.

89

"Now we just need to find WEAPONS-U-LIKE," said Icky.

Icky and Stinky began wandering round the shops. It seemed strange that although everything was free, no one seemed interested in shopping. All they wanted to do was hug each other, and hug Icky and Stinky, and say "See you at the party!"

"I hope this stops soon," said Stinky, "I'm getting worn away with hugging."

"Do you see what I see?" said Icky. Up ahead was a mammoth superstore:

TANKS FOR NOTHING

"At last!" cried Stinky.

The two great mates marched into the store. There was a big circular desk in the centre, with a very tall woman standing behind it.

"We'd like a tank, please!" said Icky.

"Of course," said the tall woman, squeezing Icky's hand. "Water tank or gas tank?"

"Battle tank," said Icky.

The woman looked confused. "Battle tank?" she said. "I've never heard of a battle tank."

"You know," said Icky. "For fighting a war."

"War?" said the woman. "What war?"

"We've come from the past," explained Stinky. "We're in the middle of a war against some pigs."

"I'll get Mrs J2," said the woman. She pressed her forehead and thought hard. Up through the floor came another woman, who seemed quite normal, except she had a pig's head.

"Can I help?" she grunted, with a warm smile.

"We've come from the past," explained Stinky. "We're in the middle of a war against … some enemies."

"We need a tank," said Icky. "A battle tank."

Mrs J2 shook her head. "I'm afraid you've made a mistake," she said.

"What kind of mistake?" asked Stinky.

"The last war was six hundred years ago," said Mrs J2.

Stinky's face dropped.

"We're all part of Blue Soup now," said the tall woman.

"We agree on everything," said Mrs J2, putting an arm around her friend.

Icky and Stinky were dumbstruck.

"You can have a water tank if you like," said Mrs J2.

"Thanks," said Stinky, "but no thanks."

"Bye," said Icky.

The two great mates sloped towards the exit, terribly depressed.

"See you at the party!" called Mrs J2.

"Whatever," said Icky.

The two great mates trudged back into the square and flopped down on a space-moss bench.

"Now what are we going to do?" said Stinky.

Icky shrugged. "Well," he said, "I suppose we *could* go to the party."

Chapter Nine

Icky and Stinky lay sprawled over the backs of two huge mountain dogs, grinning like idiots.

"That blue chocolate was *tasty!*" said Stinky.

"That water-bouncing was *ducks deluxe!*" said Icky.

There was no question about it. Icky and Stinky were at the best party in the history of the universe. They lay at the edge of a massive arena which towered up to the heavens, full of noise, light and delight. If they wanted to dance, they could jump about in a huge live-in picture screen. If they wanted to eat, they could bounce over to a thousand tables of treats. The music was sensational, and the lights and smells were even better.

"Do you think they have parties like this every day?" asked Stinky.

"Maybe," said Icky, "or maybe it's someone's birthday."

"I'm starting to like the year 3000," said Stinky.

"Even if there aren't any tanks," said Icky.

A bunch of pig-heads went by. They all gave Icky and Stinky a hug. Icky and Stinky hugged them back.

"I've been thinking," said Stinky.

"Yes?" said Icky.

"Wouldn't it be nice," said Stinky, "to stay here?"

"I'd been thinking that," said Icky.

A huge swing full of dancing people swept past them. They all waved at Icky and Stinky. Icky and Stinky waved back.

"I did promise my uncle I'd look after the house," said Stinky.

"Bryan's looking after it," said Icky.

"True," said Stinky, "but he is kind of expecting us back."

"I'll text him," said Icky.

"Do you think that'll work?" said Stinky.

"Course it will," said Icky. "I'll say, 'if u want us back, txt us'. So if we don't hear from him, we'll know it's all right to stay."

"Good thinking," said Stinky. "I feel better about it now." He gave his mountain dog a little tap on the shoulder. "How's it going, M8?" he said.

"Nearly time now," said M8.

"Nearly time?" said Stinky. "Nearly time for what?"

Suddenly there was a loud announcement: "One minute to go!"

"Eh?" said Icky.

"Fifty-nine!" went the crowd. "Fifty-eight! Fifty-seven!"

"Is it New Year?" asked Stinky.

M8 and the second dog laughed. "You don't know?" they asked.

"Know what?" asked Stinky.

"About the comet," replied M8.

"What comet?" asked Stinky.

"That comet!" said M8, pointing at the sky, where a huge flaming ball was streaming towards them.

"It's going to hit us!" cried Icky.

"That's right," said M8. "It's going to put a complete end to life as we know it."

"Fifty-two!" cried the crowd. "Fifty-one!"

"Not to worry," said M8. "We're OK about death. We understand it."

Icky and Stinky stared at each other, mouths open. "Run, Stinky!" cried Icky. The two great mates leapt off the dogs and ran like blazes.

"We love you!" called M8.

"Whatever!" cried Icky.

Icky and Stinky had never run so fast. They arrived panting at the nearest bubble station, only to find the station empty and the bubbles standing still. This was perhaps not surprising, seeing as the world was about to end.

"Oh no!" cried Icky.

"We're doomed!" cried Stinky.

At this point the two great mates had the most amazing piece of luck. As I have mentioned before, Stinky's pants contained a whole mass of life-forms. Under the huge heat of the asteroid, these life-forms were getting very agitated and giving off various gases.

Suddenly the heat set light to the gases and Stinky took off like a rocket, with Icky hanging on for grim death. The two of them flew at fantastic speed across the city, tumbling down a few yards short of the hill where they had arrived. Slightly dazed, they sprinted up the hill, leapt into the van, and clicked on their seat belts.

"Go!" said Icky.

"Where?" said Stinky.

"Anywhere!" said Icky.

Stinky pushed the slider back as far as it would

go and pressed the green button. They just about heard the C of a humungous CRASH, then there was nothing but a pleasant hum.

Note from Blue Soup:

Perhaps you find this episode difficult to believe. If so, you probably don't know much about science. Many gases explode, including gases produced by human beings. The Spoonheads were very concerned about this. They thought about changing the way humans digest, but decided against it, because then they'd have nothing to laugh about.

"Are we there yet?" asked Icky.

"How can I say if we're there," replied Stinky, "when I don't know where we're going?"

"Can't we reset the control?" asked Icky.

"It won't move," replied Stinky.

It really was a long journey this time, even longer than the first one. There was nothing to do but wait and hope – except that Icky was no good at waiting, and Stinky was no good at hoping. At last, however, the hum stopped and the screens came down at the windows. A thin light came in, but they seemed to be right in the thick of something.

"It's definitely not the house," said Stinky.

"It looks like a jungle," said Icky.

Icky and Stinky struggled out of the time van. There was no sign of a city. There was no sign of people. In fact, there was nothing but ferns.

"Do you think we're still in the future?" asked Stinky.

"I wouldn't bet on it," said Icky.

The two great mates decided to explore. There was no point in going home without *something* to fight the pigs with. They struggled through the ferns in search of helpful people or an abandoned battle tank.

"Let's play I-Spy," suggested Icky.

"OK," said Stinky. "I spy, with my little eye, something beginning with F."

"Ferns," replied Icky.

"Well done," said Stinky. "Your go."

"I spy, with my little eye," said Icky, "something beginning with F."

Stinky ummed and erred for several minutes and

finally shook his head. "I'm no good at this game," he said. "Let's play something else."

"Let's play shouting," suggested Icky.

Shouting was Icky's favourite game. The game involved making as much noise as possible, and Icky was very good at it. He bent his knees, cupped his hands round his mouth and put his whole body and soul into every yell. Usually cats and dogs bolted and birds fled in a mad flapping of wings. This time, however, nothing moved.

"Do you think there's *anything* here?" wondered Stinky.

"I've just spotted something," said Icky.

There was a brown hill in the middle of the ferns. Icky led the way there. "If we climb up on here," he said, "we might find out where we are."

Icky and Stinky climbed the small hill. It felt strange under their feet – slightly warm, and a little bit bouncy.

"Let's play trampolines!" said Icky.

Icky and Stinky started bouncing around like nutters. Suddenly there was a groan.

"What was that?" said Stinky.

"It seemed to come from underneath us," said Icky.

To Icky and Stinky's amazement, the hill began to rise beneath their feet.

Up it went …

… and up …

… and up some more.

"W-w-what's that?" stammered Stinky.

Stinky pointed forward. The hill seemed to be growing a head. The head swayed one way and another on a long rubbery neck.

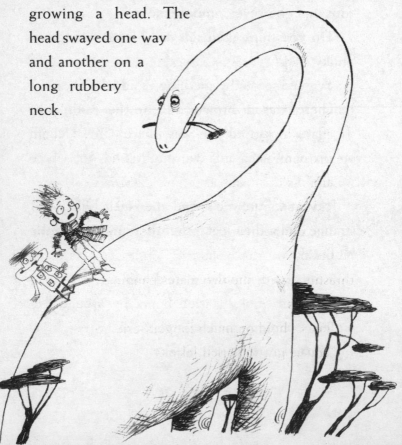

Then it turned right round, and Icky and Stinky had the shock of their lives.

The two great mates were face to face with a dinosaur.

"Werrr!" cried Stinky. "What do we do now?"

The dinosaur opened its mouth and let out a roar like a ten-megaton hair drier. It was lucky for Icky he couldn't smell its breath. Compared to the dinosaur, Stinky was a sweetly scented rose.

The dinosaur really didn't like having two boys on its back. It began to thrash about, lashing its massive tail at Icky and Stinky. The two mates hung on like rodeo riders on a bucking bull.

"Hang on, Stinky!" cried Icky. "If we fall off, we're dogmeat!"

"Unless it's a plant-eater!" cried Stinky.

"I don't want to find out!" cried Icky.

The dinosaur was geting madder by the second. It began to run about in circles, roaring and thrashing, with the two mates hanging on by their fingernails.

"I can't hold on much longer!" cried Stinky.

"You've got to!" cried Icky.

There seemed to be no way of escape. Then Icky spotted something, far off in the sky. "Is that a hang-glider?" he said.

Stinky screwed up his eyes. "I think you're right!" he said.

"A caveman, in a hang-glider!" said Icky excitedly.

"Coming to our rescue!" cried Stinky.

Icky and Stinky waved their arms frantically. "Over here!" they cried.

The hang-glider veered towards them.

"He's seen us!" cried Icky.

The hang-glider came faster and faster, homing in like a missile. Suddenly, however, there was a horrible screech, and Stinky realised their terrible mistake. It wasn't a hang-glider at all. It was a pterodactyl, which in case you don't know, was a flying dinosaur.

"Watch out, Icky!" cried Stinky, but it was too late. Icky was snatched in the great beast's claws, then carried up, up, up into the sky, until finally he vanished from sight.

Everything seemed to go very quiet. At first, Stinky couldn't quite believe what had happened.

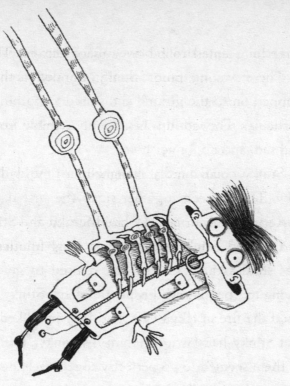

Then the awful truth sank in. Stinky slid off the side of the dinosaur and dropped to the ground.

The dinosaur's fearsome head turned.

Stinky sat on the ground, not bothering to move. "Go on," he said. "Eat me. See if I care."

The dinosaur opened its gaping mouth, and crunched down on a fern. Stinky gave a little laugh, but not a happy one. He wandered off, in no particular direction, then broke into a jog, then started to run. He had to find Icky, and do something fantastically brave to save him, but what?

There was no point. Stinky stopped running, flopped on to the ground and stared at nothing in particular. The world was suddenly terribly lonely, and sad, and no longer home.

Stinky could hardly remember a time without Icky. They'd been together since the first day at nursery school, when Icky had sneezed and Stinky had offered him a hanky. Even though the hanky was solid as a rock, Icky had refused to give up trying to open it with his plastic pliers. Stinky had liked the fire in Icky's eyes, and Icky had liked the fact Stinky had just given him his hanky. The two of them seemed to go perfectly together, like roast beef and mustard. Or, if you're a plant-eater, like lentils and coconut.

The sun set and the ancient Earth went dark. Stinky followed the trail of broken ferns back towards the time van. It felt terrible not to have done *anything* to save Icky, or at least *tried*, in the hope of a miracle. But, as you already know, Stinky was not much good at hoping.

Stinky reached the van. "Goodbye, best mate," he said. He waved forlornly at the sky and climbed in.

Icky was sitting on the front seat, dripping wet, cradling a large egg.

"Icky!" cried Stinky. "You're alive!"

Icky pulled his lucky feather from his pocket. "Uncle Jav was right," he said. "It did save my life."

"But how?" gasped Stinky.

"Dinosaurs may be big," said Icky, "but they're also ticklish."

"Of course!" said Stinky.

"Mind you," said Icky, "it was lucky I fell in the water."

Stinky's eyes went to the egg. "What's that you've got there?" he asked.

"I don't know," said Icky. "I found it by the pond."

"It's a big egg," said Stinky.

"I thought we could throw it at the pigs," said Icky.

A weary feeling came over Stinky. He had forgotten about the pigs. "I suppose we'd better go back," he said.

"Guess so," said Icky.

Icky shoved the egg up his jumper and pulled on his seat belt. The two great mates set the slider very carefully. Then they were off, out of the age of the dinosaurs, back to the age of Blue Soup and angry pigs. Stinky felt fantastic to be back alongside Icky, but a terrible wave of guilt was coming over him.

"I wanted to rescue you," he said, "but I couldn't think of what to do."

"I'm sure you tried your best," said Icky.

"I didn't do *anything*," said Stinky.

Icky said it didn't matter, but it mattered to Stinky. The further they travelled, the worse he felt. By the time the machine stopped he felt like the lowest being in the universe.

"I wonder where we are now?" asked Icky.

They soon found out. As the shields came down, Bryan was already at the window, and he looked desperate. "Where have you been?" he cried.

"Oh, here and there," said Icky.

"Have you got a weapon?" asked Bryan anxiously.

Icky pulled up his jumper and produced the egg.

"*That's* a weapon?" cried Bryan.

"Yes, it is!" said Icky defiantly.

"The door's going to give way any second," said Bryan, "and all you've got is …" Bryan stopped. He studied the egg more closely. "Where did you get this?" he asked.

"Why?" asked Icky.

"It looks like a dinosaur egg," said Bryan.

"How do you know?" asked Icky.

"Because I know everything," said Bryan.

Icky threw back his shoulders and stood as tall as he could. "Yes," he said. "It is a dinosaur egg, and we're going to hatch it, and make a dinosaur."

"How do you propose to do that?" scoffed Bryan.

Icky looked around for inspiration. His eyes fell on the seat belt, and lit up. "We're going to put it in the time van," he said, "and not put on the seat belt!"

Stinky stirred from his awful gloom. "Do

you think that would work?" he asked.

"Of course it'll work!" said Icky.

"I'll believe it when I see it," said Bryan.

Note from Blue Soup:
I won't bother explaining this. Remember rule 89.

There was a huge THUMP at the front door of the house. Bryan shuddered. Stinky jumped out of the time van and Icky quickly placed the egg on the front seat. "Here goes," he said. He stabbed the On button and jumped clear.

The time van came to life. It hummed, it rattled and it throbbed.

"How are we going to stop it?" asked Stinky.

"I hadn't thought of that," said Icky.

There was no way of knowing what was going on inside the van. Suddenly, however, something dramatic started to happen to the outside of it.

The sides started to swell.

Little splits appeared around the edges.

The whole thing began to creak.

And then ...

KER-RACK!

The time van splintered into a hundred pieces, and there stood a twenty-ton dinosaur, bright blue, with a jagged crest around its neck and two massive curving horns. For a moment it seemed dazed. Then it shook itself, let out a huge throaty groan, and began thundering around the little garage in search of a way out.

Bryan cowered in terror. Icky jumped into the nearest cupboard. But Stinky stood quite still. This time, he really would save his friend. As the dinosaur crashed past, he seized hold of its crest and held on for grim death. Bit by bit he clambered up on to its neck, till he was riding it like a jockey. "Woah, boy!" he cried.

The dinosaur was not interested in being tamed. It pounded and groaned and thumped into the walls.

"Woah!" cried Stinky. "Woah!"

With all the strength he could muster, he yanked on the dinosaur till it was facing the garage doors. Then he dug his heels hard into its sides. The dinosaur gave a mighty screech, lowered its horns, and charged ...

Meanwhile, outside, General Pig was also giving the order to charge. With a shrill yell, the army of pigs raced up the slope towards the house …

… just as Stinky, the dinosaur, and half a garage door came smashing out of it.

"NO!" cried the pigs.

"Go!" cried Stinky.

"Hold the line!" cried General Pig.

General Pig's words were in vain. The pigs scattered in terror. Stinky flew after them, urging the raging dinosaur this way and that. They smashed the catapult, flattened the army's tents, and sent showers of ice and snow after the fleeing pigs. Icky and Bryan raced out behind, wielding frying pans on sticks. But Stinky really didn't need any help. He chased the pigs all the way to the woods, then leapt off just as the dinosaur went crashing through the trees.

What happened to the dinosaur they would never know. But one thing was for sure: the army of pigs would never bother them again.

"You did it, Stinky!" said Icky. "You saved the house!"

"Am I a hero now?" asked Stinky, slightly dazed.

"You're a superstar," said Icky.

"Oh good," said Stinky. "I feel better now."

Bryan came up to them. He was carrying the general's hat. "I found this by the front door," he said.

"But the pigs never got to the front door," said Stinky. He pointed to the woods. "They went that way."

"Was the general with them?" asked Bryan.

"Come to think of it," said Stinky, "no."

The three great mates looked back towards the open front door.

"Uh-oh," said Bryan.

"He's got into the house!" said Stinky.

"Quick!" cried Icky.

The three great mates sprinted past the abandoned catapult, up the steps, and into the house. Bryan checked the bedrooms, Icky checked the dressing-up room, and Stinky checked the kitchen. They met up back in the living room, panting for breath.

"No sign of him!" they all said.

Icky's eyes darted round the living room. "Hang on," he said. "Who turned the telly on?"

"Not me," said Stinky.

"Not me," said Bryan.

Everyone looked at the sofa. There, next to Dronezone, was a fifth potato, with an odd mark which looked just like an eye-patch.

Chapter Ten

Icky and Stinky sat on their favourite tree stumps, on the edge of the silver forest, on a warm winter afternoon. Icky was watching the city slowly appear through the melting snow. Stinky was just waking from a quiet doze.

"I've just had the most amazing dream," said Stinky.

"What was it about?" asked Icky.

"Well," said Stinky, "we went to see my uncle, and he had this house, and then a pig came to the door—"

"Stinky," said Icky, "that wasn't a dream. That was real."

"Real, was it?" said Stinky. He puzzled for a while. "What about the Spoonheads?" he asked.

"Were they a dream?"

"Nope," said Icky. "They're real too."

Stinky puzzled for a while longer. "What about when I was walking down the High Street," he said, "and the giant fish fell on me?"

"That *was* a dream," said Icky.

"Oh good," said Stinky.

There was a long silence.

"I can't wait to get back to the house," said Icky.

"You're going back?" asked Stinky.

"Course I am!" said Icky. "Aren't you?"

"I wasn't going to," said Stinky.

"But you promised your uncle you'd look after it!" said Icky.

"I thought Bryan could look after it," said Stinky.

"We'll *all* look after it," said Icky.

Stinky considered this. "It's not much of an Aim In Life," he said, "looking after a house."

Icky jumped to his feet. "We'll make it the greatest house in the universe," he said. "We'll invite everyone to stay, and we'll have new adventures every day, and we'll call it Stinky Finger's House of Fun!"

"Hmm," said Stinky. "I like the name."

"We'll put it over the door," said Icky.

"In coloured lights?" asked Stinky.

"If you like," said Icky.

There was another silence.

"Race you down," said Stinky.

Another title from Hodder Children's Books:

THE DEADLY SECRET OF DOROTHY W.

Jon Blake

When Jasmin wins a place at the Dorothy Wordsearch School for Gifted Young Writers, things look fishy. Who exactly is the mysterious Mr Collins?

How come Miss Birdshot, the wizened old housekeeper, is so incredibly strong?

And why do Jasmin's fellow pupils keep disappearing?

As Jasmin unravels Dorothy W.'s deadly secret, she finds herself literally writing for her life. Now, only the most brilliant story will help her survive!

'It's original and witty, full of amusing characterisation — a funny adventure story which credits its readers with intelligence.' Books for Keeps

Another title from Hodder Children's Books:

THE MAD MISSION OF JASMIN J.

Jon Blake

The last time Jasmin saw Dorothy Wordsearch, the awful author was being eaten by a monster.

So how come she's still writing stories?

It's time for Jasmin to investigate – helped, but mainly hindered, by her hyper sidckick Kevin Shilling.

And when Kevin is won over by a sinister new enemy, Jasmin will need all her wits to save him from a terrible fate …